What did your Dinosaur do today?

WRITTEN BY TIFFANY TUTU

ILLUSTRATED BY CHRISARA DESIGNS

MW01094884

Copyright © – Books of a Feather, LLC – 2020
All Artwork © – Books of a Feather, LLC – 2020
All Rights Reserved

No part of this publication may be reproduced in any form or stored, transmitted or
recorded by any means without the written permission of the author.
This is a work of fiction.

Published by Kids Book Press
An imprint of A & S Publishing, A & S Holmes, Inc.
Sharon Kizziah-Holmes – Publishing Coordinator

ISBN: 978-1-951772-40-6

DEDICATION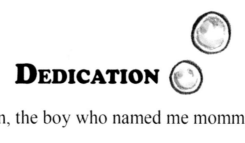

For Brigden, the boy who named me mommy.

Did your dinosaur
sit on a swing,

or build a fort fit for a king?

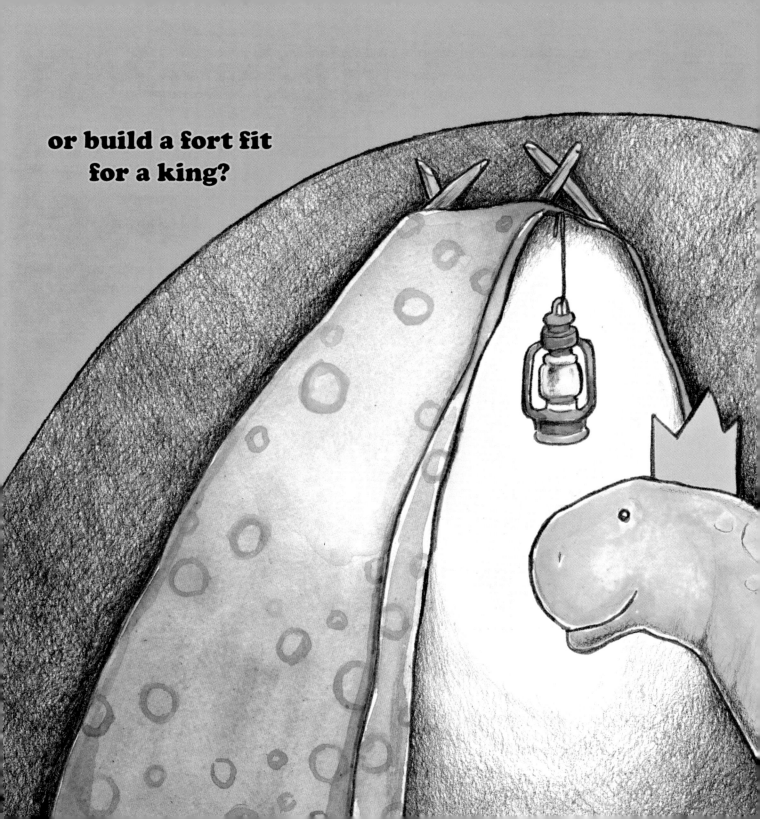

Did your dinosaur learn to spell his name,

or draw a picture for a moment of fame?

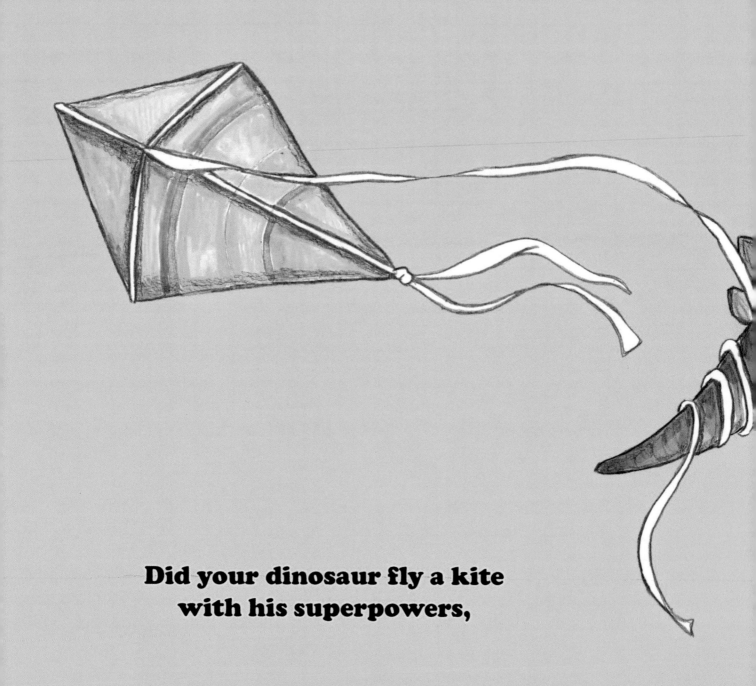

Did your dinosaur fly a kite
with his superpowers,

**or give his mom
fresh cut flowers?**

Did your dinosaur drive a train,

or look out the window and watch the rain?

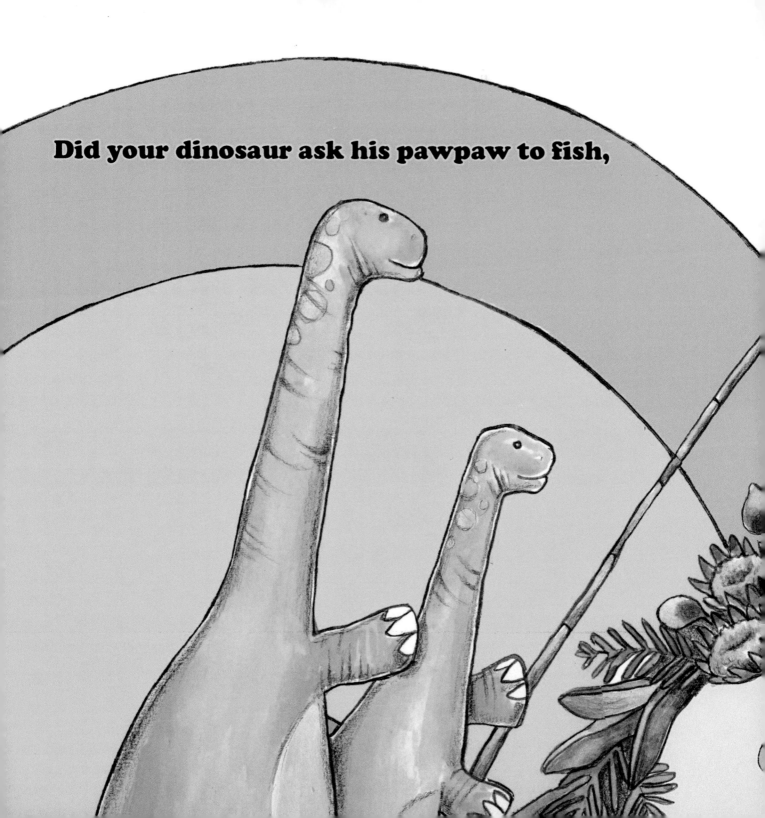

Did your dinosaur ask his pawpaw to fish,

or look for bugs that they could squish?

Did your dinosaur make a s'more,

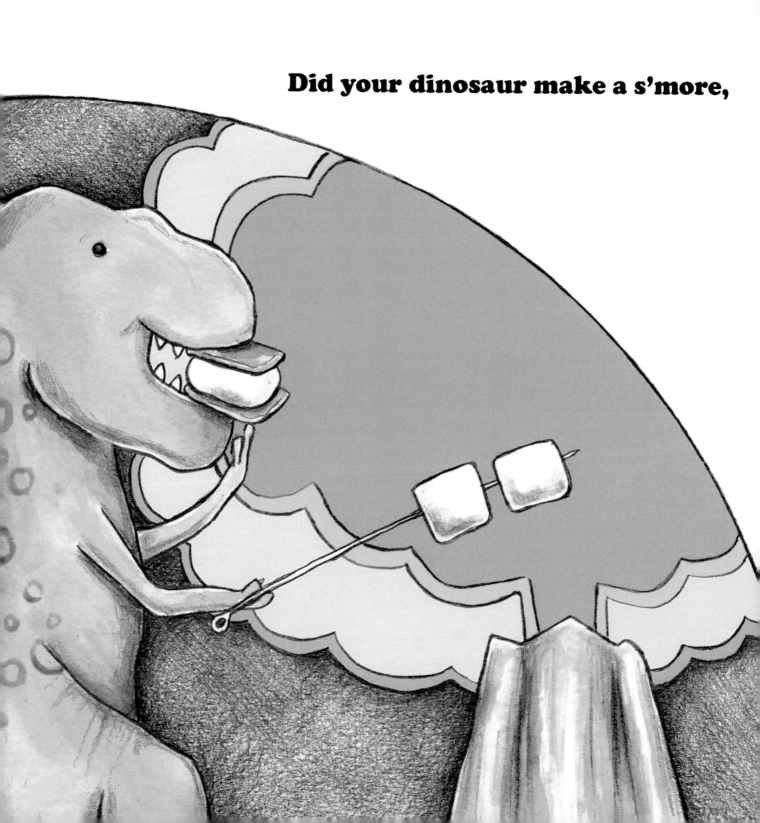

or build a sandcastle
on the seashore?

Did your dinosaur ride his bike,

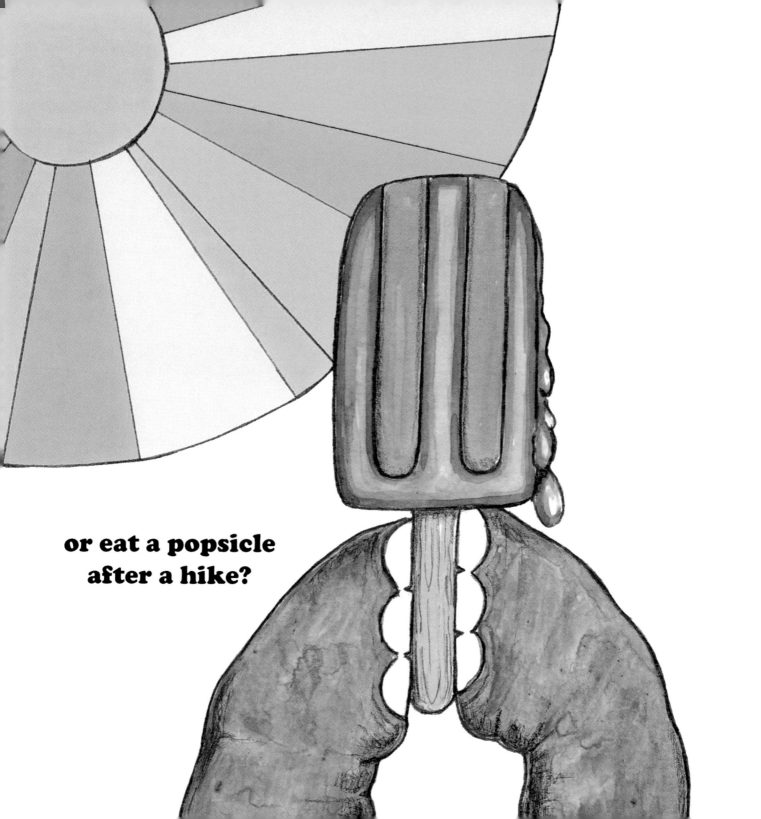

or eat a popsicle
after a hike?

Did your dinosaur wish for a friend,

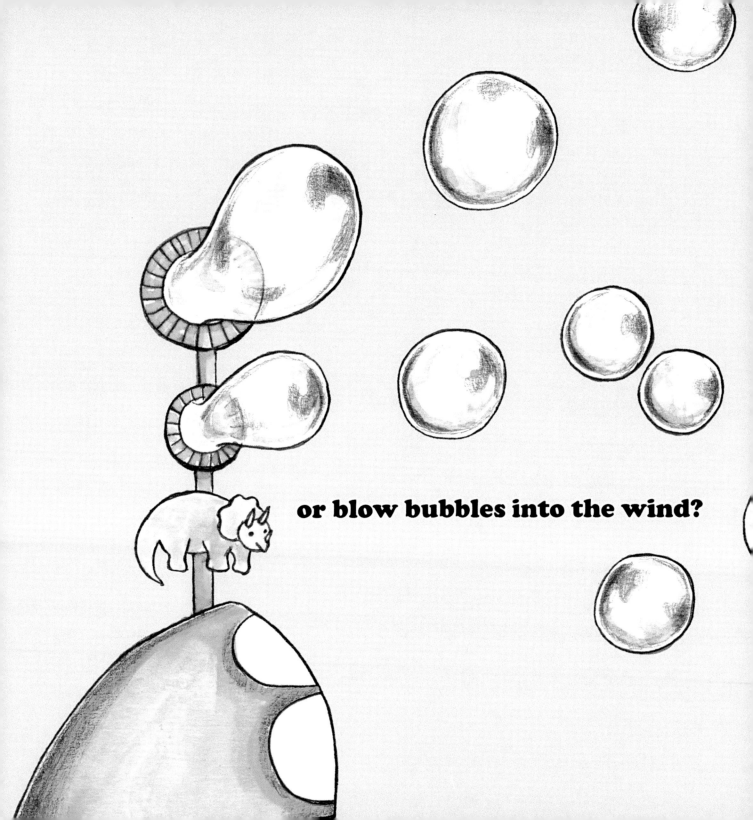

**Did your dinosaur make
up his own dance,**

or fly an airplane
all the way to France?

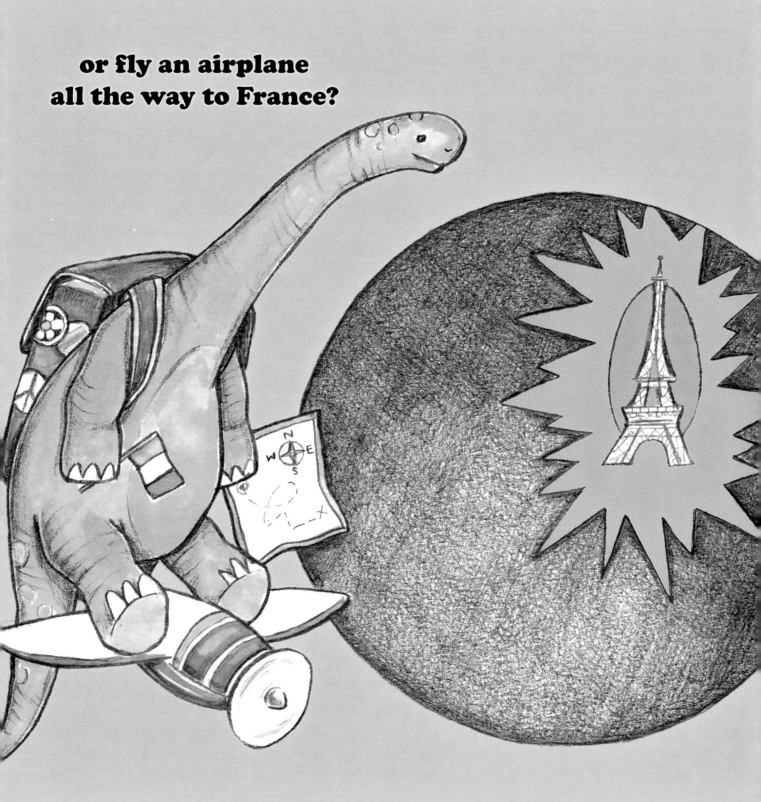

Did your
dinosaur
pee on
the potty,

or play in the mud and try not to be naughty?

Did your dinosaur go sledding in the snow,

**or tie his sister's
hair in a bow?**

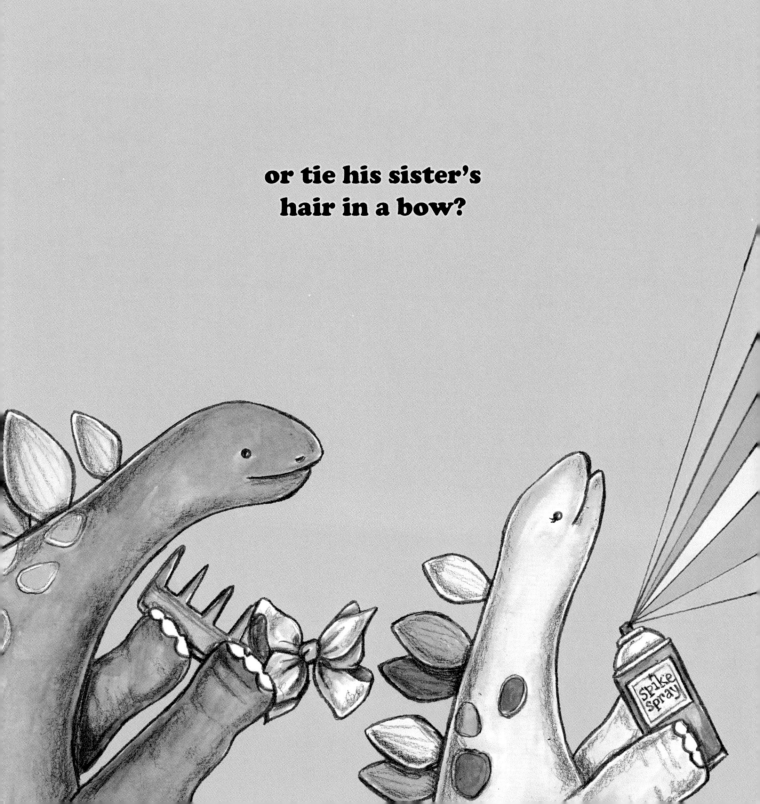

Did your dinosaur eat his fruit,

or hide his veggies
inside his boot?

Did your dinosaur
ask for a hug,

or drink root beer
from a mug?

Did your dinosaur say, "I love you"?

I bet he did,

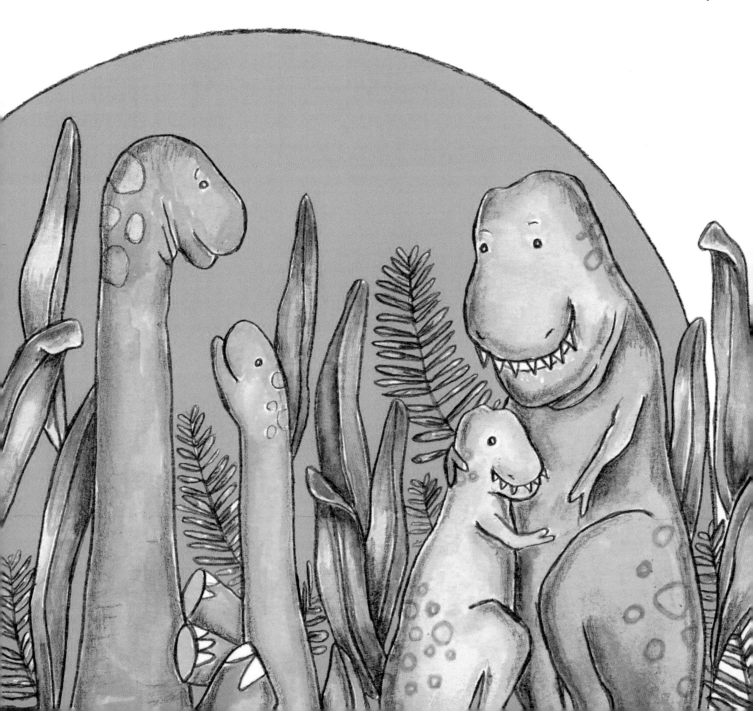

and I love you, too!

ACKNOWLEDGEMENTS

A dream written in my heart, transcribed to paper.

To my son, Brigden, my inspiration for this book. You cuddled next to me while I wrote,
a memory I will never forget.

To my stepdaughter, Ashlyn. I rediscovered my love of storytelling when you came into my life.

To my daughter, Livianah. This book will live as a reminder that little girl dreams really do come true.

To my husband, Dave. You are the answer to endless prayers. I love you.

To my dad, Dusty. You created my fondest childhood memories by reading countless books at bedtime.

To my mom, Della. Your sacrifice and love for me is unmatched.

To the illustrators, Sara and Christa. You transformed my words into beautiful images of life. I am forever
in awe of your God given talent. May you never tire of using your gift to touch hearts.

To my mother-in-law, Carol. You inspire me to grow and cover me in prayer. You gave me a blue notebook
and told me to write; I did.

To Gabrielle Martin, author of *Hold My Hand, Mama*. Thank you for taking the time to answer my
questions. You didn't know me, but you chose to invest in me regardless. I am thankful for the kindness
of strangers.

To Sharon, at *Paperback Press Publishing*. You seamlessly guided me through the publishing process.
Without you, this book would still be in my little blue notebook.

To God. Thank you for placing a dream in a little girl's heart and for keeping the dream alive year after
year. Thank you for giving me a season of stillness, without it I may have never taken the time to make
the dream come to life.

ABOUT THE AUTHOR

Tiffany Tutu wrote her first children's book when she was a child herself. Her first editor, her mother, Della, instilled belief in Tiffany that she could be a children's author one day. The dream laid dormant until Tiffany became a mother. With the pen name of Tiffany Tutu, a nickname given to her by her kindergarten teacher, she was inspired by the small moments and memories she collected during quarantine with her son, Brigden, to write a book celebrating him and those moments.

She lives in the Midwest with her husband, three children, a cat that doesn't age, endless dinosaurs, countless babydolls, and a few tutus, of course.

A common saying is that nothing in life is certain, but when it comes to Tiffany, one can be assured she has a glass of tea in hand, no socks on her feet, and a dream growing in her heart.

She can be found online at tiffanytutu.com or on Instagram at @AuthorTiffanyTutu.

ABOUT THE ILLUSTRATORS

Twin sisters, Christa Schmitz Tiggemann & Sara Schmitz Olson are the creatives behind *Chrisara Designs*.

Springfield, MO based, the twins have produced art and design for many companies and individuals. They share a love for nature, animals, pretty color combinations, and the 70's era which have influenced a lot of their work. You can view some of their previous projects on Instagram at @Chrisaradesigns

Made in the USA
Coppell, TX
29 March 2021

52662660R00021